First American Edition 2007
by Kane/Miller Book Publishers, Inc.
La Jolla, California

First published in 2004 by BIR, Seoul, Korea under the title *The Zoo*
Copyright © 2004 by Suzy Lee

Kane Miller, A Division of EDC Publishing
P.O. Box 470663
Tulsa, OK 74147-0663
www.kanemiller.com
www.edcpub.com

Library of Congress Control Number: 2006931563
Printed and bound in China by Regent Publishing Services, Ltd.
2 3 4 5 6 7 8 9 10
ISBN: 978-1-933605-28-9

THE ZOO

SUZY LEE

Kane Miller
A DIVISION OF EDC PUBLISHING

I went to the zoo with my mom and dad.

We visited the monkey house,

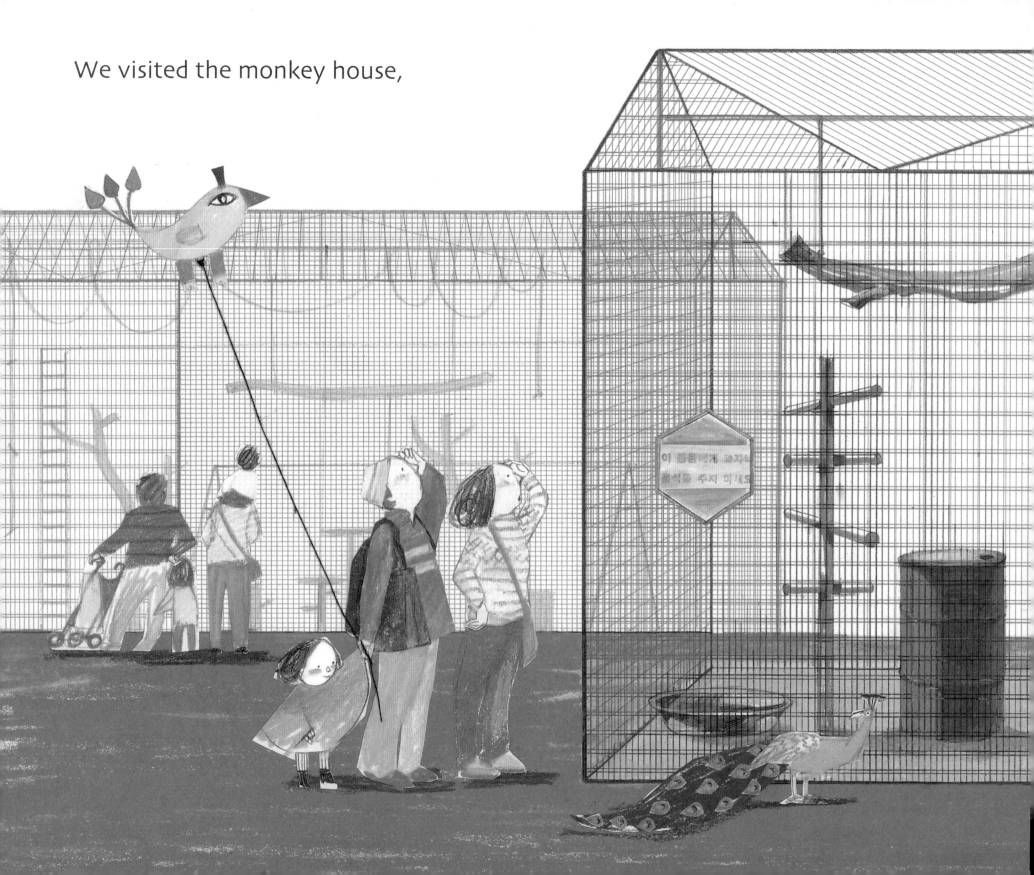

and Bear Hill.

We watched the hippos in their pool,

…and went to the elephants.

We saw the giraffes, too.

We visited the aviary,

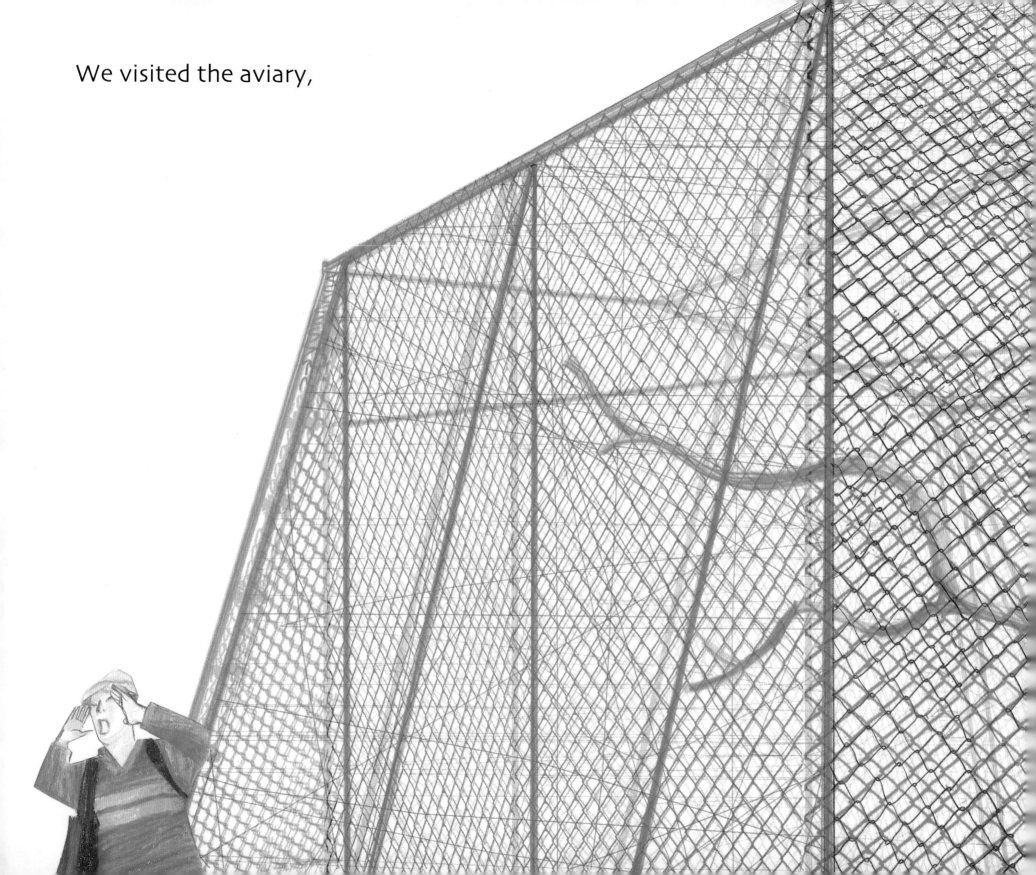

and then the gorillas.

I love the zoo. It's very exciting.

Mom and Dad think so too.